Other titles in the series:

978 1 4451 4166 4

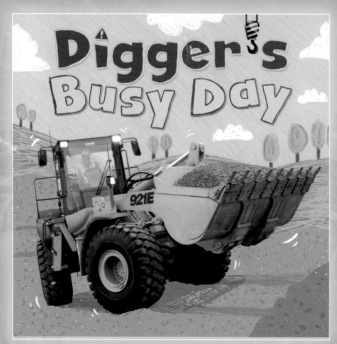

978 1 4451 4311 8

978 1 4451 4315 6

www.franklinwatts.co.uk

Franklin Watts
First published in Great Britain in 2015 by The Watts Publishing Group

Picture credits: Chukov/Shutterstock: 15; Clark and Company/istockphoto: 5bl, 29bc.; John Deere: 3,
8-9, 22-23; Peter Elvidge/Shutterstock: 29c; Gannet77/istockphoto: 5br; Eric Gevaert/
Shutterstock: 28b; Jessmine/Shutterstock: 6-7; Denise Kappa/Shutterstock: 18-19; Peter
Macdiarmid/Getty Images: 16-17; Mikhail Malyshev/Shutterstock: 24-25; mikeledray/Shutterstock:
10; Cameron Pasnak/istockphoto: back cover, 5ct, 20-21; Pavelk/Shutterstock: 4cr.
sanddebeautheil/Shutterstock: 12-13; Shutterstock: 29r; Taina Sohlman/Shutterstock: 26.

Series Editor: Melanie Palmer
Designer & Illustrator: Dan Bramall
Design Manager: Peter Scoulding
Picture researcher: Diana Morris

Every attempt has been made to clear copyright. Should there be any inadvertent
omission please apply to the publisher for rectification.

ISBN 978 1 4451 4319 4 (hbk)
ISBN 978 1 4451 4321 7 (pbk)
ISBN 978 1 4451 4320 0 (library ebook)
Printed in China

Franklin Watts
An imprint of
Hachette Children's Group
Part of The Watts Publishing Group
Carmelite House
50 Victoria Embankment
London EC4Y 0DZ

An Hachette UK Company
www.hachette.co.uk

Tractor's Farmyard Fun

Written by Amelia Marshall

Illustrated by Dan Bramall

W

FRANKLIN WATTS

LONDON · SYDNEY

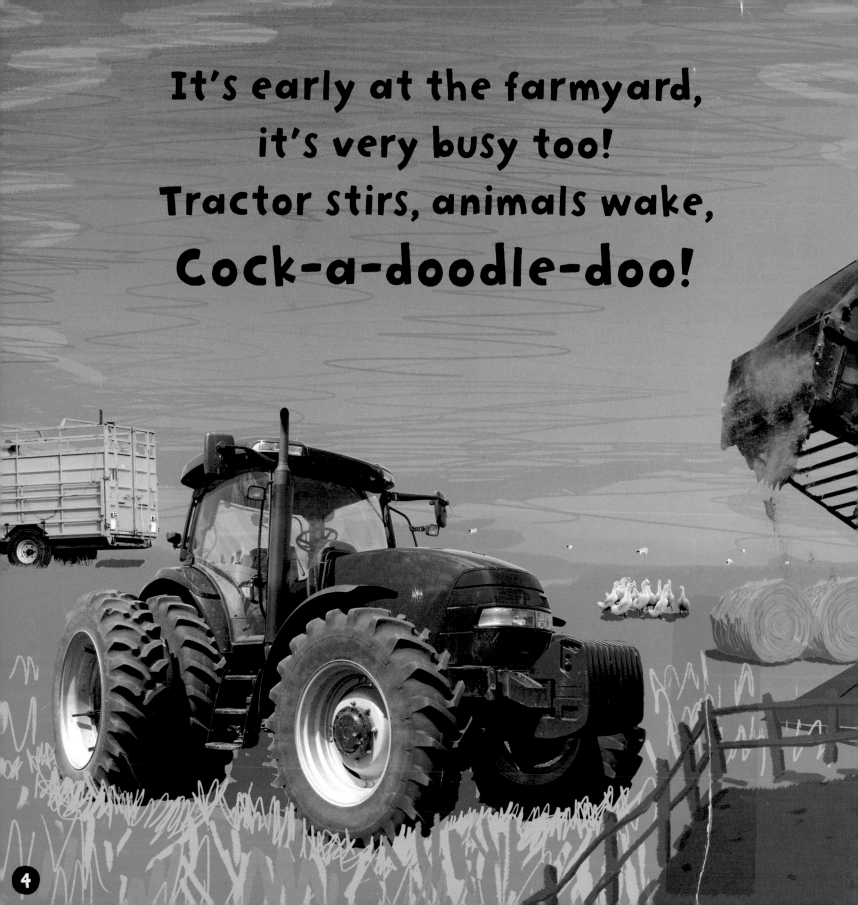

It's early at the farmyard,
it's very busy too!
Tractor stirs, animals wake,
Cock-a-doodle-doo!

Big baler begins to **WHIRR**,
its engine **HUMS** away.
The animals need feeding,
the horses want their hay!

Red tractor rolls along
as its heavy tyres **THUD**,
chug, chug, chugging
across the fields of mud.

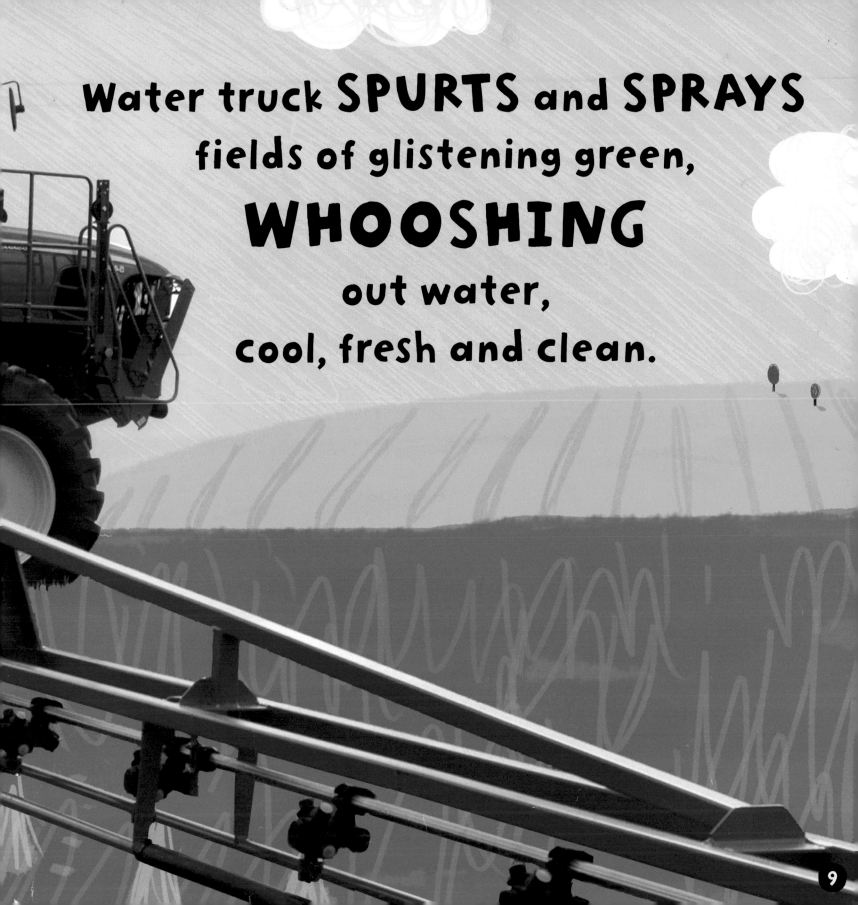

Water truck **SPURTS** and **SPRAYS**
fields of glistening green,
WHOOSHING
out water,
cool, fresh and clean.

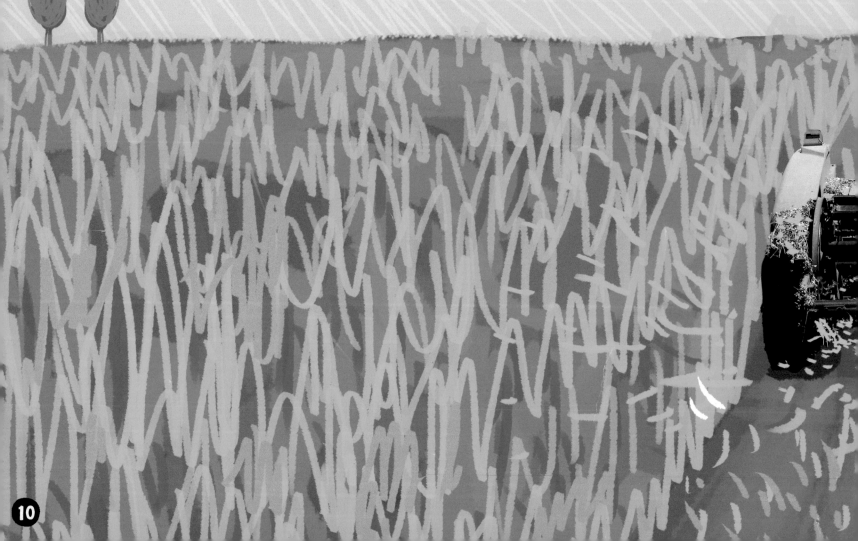

Tractor's grass cutter
is **GULPING UP** the grass,
spitting out sticks and stems,
blades **CUTTING** fast.

Tractor tugs its trailer,
trampling and **trundling,**

Cows are going up and down, **bouncing** and **bumbling.**

Busy blue tractor
is **BIG** and **STRONG**,
HEAVING the heavy
plough along.

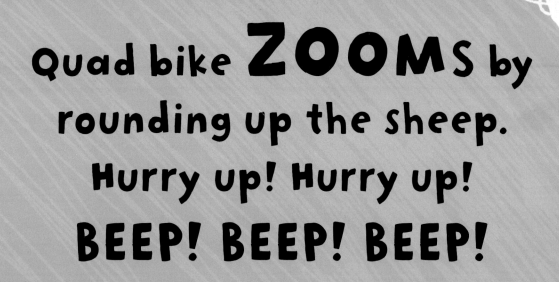

Quad bike **ZOOM**s by
rounding up the sheep.
Hurry up! Hurry up!
BEEP! BEEP! BEEP!

Hungry combine harvester
gobbles up the grain,
CHOPPING and **CHOMPING**
again and again.

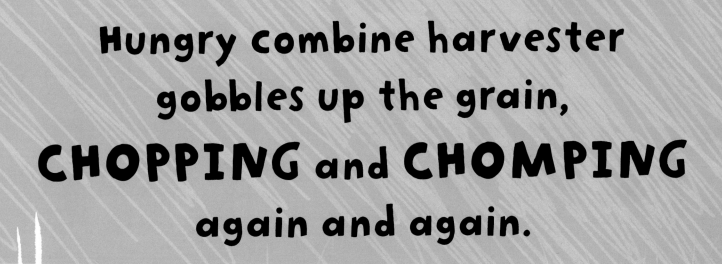

Hay baler **SPINS** the hay,
all the straw is turning.
Bales fly out underneath,
whirling and
swirling.

Tractor's fork
is stretching **HIGH!**
Lifting bales
up, up to the sky!

SWISH

This busy blue tractor
goes BRRMM, VRRMM,
ZOOM!
Piling up the hefty bales

with a
BOOM, BOOM, BOOM!

Clickety
Clack

This crawler tractor
has special non-stick **tracks.**
It moves over muddy **bumps**
with a **clickety-clack!**

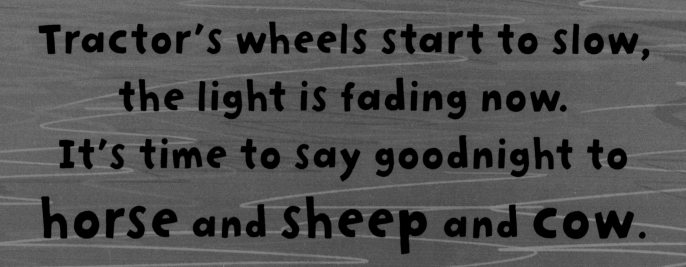

Tractor's wheels start to slow,
the light is fading now.
It's time to say goodnight to
horse and sheep and cow.

All the tractors slowly stop,
red and green and blue,
as all the engines gently hum,
goodnight to them and you!

Tractor terms

Grille – vents to help air keep the engine cool.

Wing mirror – allows the driver to see what is behind.

Cab – where the driver sits.

Trailer – can attach to a tractor to carry objects or animals.

Combine harvester – cuts and separates grains and stalks.

Plough – cuts into the muddy earth and digs it up.

Bale fork – metal fork to help tractors lift and carry hay bales.

Tracks – these help the tractor not to sink in the mud.